P9-EFI-473

TAKEDOWN

Also by Rich Wallace

Winning Season Series

WINNING SEASON

TAKEDOWN

RICH WALLACE

VIKING

Boca Raton Public Library, Boca Raton, FL

VIKING
Published by Penguin Group
Penguin Young Readers Group, 345 Hudson Street, New York, New York 10014, U.S.A.
Penguin Group (Canada), 90 Eglinton Avenue East, Suite 700, Toronto, Ontario, Canada M4P 2Y3
(a division of Pearson Penguin Canada Inc.)
Penguin Books Ltd, 80 Strand, London WC2R 0RL, England
Penguin Ireland, 25 St Stephen's Green, Dublin 2, Ireland (a division of Penguin Books Ltd)
Penguin Group (Australia), 250 Camberwell Road, Camberwell, Victoria 3124, Australia
(a division of Pearson Australia Group Pty Ltd)
Penguin Books India Pvt Ltd, 11 Community Centre, Panchsheel Park, New Delhi - 110 017, India
Penguin Group (NZ), Cnr Airborne and Rosedale Roads, Albany, Auckland 1310, New Zealand
(a division of Pearson New Zealand Ltd)
Penguin Books (South Africa) (Pty) Ltd, 24 Sturdee Avenue, Rosebank, Johannesburg 2196, South Africa

Penguin Books Ltd, Registered Offices: 80 Strand, London WC2R 0RL, England
First published in 2006 by Viking, a division of Penguin Young Readers Group

1 3 5 7 9 10 8 6 4 2

Copyright © Rich Wallace, 2006
All rights reserved
LIBRARY OF CONGRESS CATALOGING-IN-PUBLICATION DATA IS AVAILABLE
ISBN: 0-670-06096-8

Printed in U.S.A.   Set in Caslon 224 Book

Without limiting the right under copyright reserved above, no part of this publication may be reproduced,
stored in or introduced into a retrieval system, or transmitted, in any form or by any means (electronic,
mechanical, photocopying, recording, or otherwise), without the prior written permission of both the
copyright owner and the above publisher of this book. The scanning, uploading, and distribution of this
book via the Internet or via any other means without the permission of the publisher is illegal and punishable
by law. Please purchase only authorized electronic editions, and do not participate in or encourage
electronic piracy of copyrighted materials. Your support of the author's rights is appreciated.

FOR LUCY

• CONTENTS •

1

Outsmarted

Could anything be harder than this?

Donald sat with his back against the gymnasium wall, eyes shut and sweat streaming down his face. His legs hurt. His shoulders ached. His left foot was starting to cramp.

He opened one eye and looked at the clock on the wall: 4:27 P.M. Coach Mills had said practice would end at 5:15. Three minutes of rest and then forty-five minutes of drills.

There was an inch of water left in his bottle, and he sucked it right down. The water was warm but it quenched his thirst a little. The corner of his mouth stung where the bottle had touched it. He put a finger to his lip. When he pulled it away, there was a dot of red. He curled his tongue to that spot and tasted blood.

I'll live, he thought.

He felt a shoe against his leg—not quite a kick, but a rather hard nudge. Freddy Salinardi was standing there, looking down at him. Freddy was a muscular eighth-grader and one of the team captains. "Let's go, wimp," he said. "Nap time is over."

Donald scrambled to his feet. Freddy called everybody wimps, at least all of the seventh-graders. This was the first day of practice, so the newcomers were getting tested by the veterans. Donald stepped toward the mat. Freddy was already hassling Mario and Kendrick, making them stand up, too.

What a jerk, Donald thought, but he'd never say that out loud.

He had already started to figure things out. Coach worked the wrestlers hard but he was a nice guy, and he certainly seemed to know his stuff about the sport.

They'd learned some basic wrestling moves earlier in the session, but the past half hour had been all about conditioning. Jumping jacks, sit-ups, running in place. Donald knew this sport would be difficult, but he hadn't envisioned anything like this.

Coach blew his whistle and quickly put the wrestlers in pairs. Donald winced when Coach lined him up with Tavo Rivera, one of the best eighth-graders. Tavo was the same size as Donald, but he was stronger and quicker.

"Wrestle!" Coach called.

Donald leaned back then lunged quickly forward, but Tavo easily sidestepped him and Donald stumbled to the mat. Tavo was on him in an instant, circling his thigh with one hand and lifting his ankle with the other. From there it was a matter of seconds until Donald was flat on his back, pinned.

Tavo was an experienced wrestler, thin with long, lean limbs and gappy teeth. He'd been a starter the previous year as a seventh-grader and now was one of the clear leaders of the team. He grinned at Donald as they got to their feet, but Donald just glared back.

"Let's go!" Donald said, spitting out the words and lunging toward Tavo again. He'd show this guy how tough he was.

Within five minutes, Tavo had pinned him four times.

Coach Mills walked over and faced Donald.

"Know what you're doing wrong?" Coach asked.

"Getting my butt kicked?" Donald said angrily.

"Yeah, you are. But why?"

"I don't know. I'm trying as hard as I can."

"Hard but not smart," Coach said. "You're giving away every move. Watch."

Coach went into a staggered stance, one foot forward, knees bent, hands out in front.

"Here's what *you* do." Coach leaned back and then lunged, just as Donald had done. "When you lean back and wind up like that, you're telling your opponent that you're about to attack. There's no surprise."

Coach went back into his stance. Then he shot forward toward Tavo, head up and his body low. "Penetrate," he said. "Take a big first step and really shoot in there toward your opponent."

Donald kept glaring at Tavo, who kept grinning back with confidence. Tavo could tell how frustrated Donald was, and he knew that his year of wrestling experience was making a huge difference.

"Got it?" Coach asked.

"Yeah," Donald said flatly.

"Then do it. There's a lot more to winning than being stronger or faster than the other wrestler. Tavo weighs the same as you, but he's outsmarting you by a mile."

"I'm smart," Donald mumbled.

"That's nice," Coach said sarcastically. "But it doesn't mean you know what you're doing yet."

Donald and Tavo circled around each other,

hands up and bodies leaning slightly forward. Tavo threw out a quick hand and Donald flinched, but Coach told him to stay low.

And quick as a flash Tavo was on him again, his hands locked behind Donald's left knee. Donald felt himself being lifted, and Tavo's shoulder was jamming into his ribs. He grabbed Tavo's back with one hand and tried to unclench the grip with the other, but suddenly both feet were in the air. He hit the mat hard. In a matter of seconds he'd been pinned for the fifth time.

Tavo stood quickly and reached down to give Donald a hand. But Donald looked away and ignored the hand. "I don't need your help," he said.

"Oh, no?" Tavo grinned confidently.

"No. And you won't be smiling when I knock you flat."

"As if that'll ever happen."

Donald didn't have a chance to reply. "Line up!" Coach called. "The fun starts now."

Donald joined the others in a straight line against the wall.

"What now?" asked Mario, tugging on Donald's scrawny arm.

Donald turned and shrugged. Mario was one of the few kids here who was shorter than Donald, but he was stockier, so they weighed about the same. His dark curly hair was matted to his forehead with sweat.

"Some new form of torture," Donald whispered.

Coach was looking over the thirty or so wrestlers, sizing them up with a smug smile. He was young—three years earlier he'd still been wrestling for the college team at Montclair State—and had the build of a solid 140-pounder.

"Nobody said this would be easy, right?" Coach said. "You new guys are getting a taste of how tough this sport is. You can't even *begin* to be a good wrestler until you get into shape. The whole key is conditioning. Without that, you're nothing."

Coach pointed to Kendrick, a quiet newcomer to Hudson City who sat next to Donald in English class. "What's your favorite sport?" he asked.

Kendrick looked around and scrunched up his mouth before answering. "Wrestling?"

"Is that a question or a statement?"

"A statement, I guess."

"Good answer."

Now Coach looked at Donald. "What's your *least* favorite sport?"

Donald put a finger to his chest as he asked weakly, "Me?"

"Yeah, you."

At this point Donald could have said "wrestling" and he wouldn't have been lying. But he said "track," which would have been true any other time. His best friend Manny Ramos was a standout distance runner, but Donald had wanted no part of that sport, despite Manny's frequent urging to join him at it.

Coach's smile got broader. "That's too bad," he said, "because guess what? Wrestlers run their butts off."

Coach made a circular motion with his hand. "Laps around the gym," he said. "A nice steady pace.

We're not racing here, just staying in motion."

There was a collective groan from the group, but all of them started jogging. The gym was small and the corners were tight, but the jogging did seem easier to Donald than all those calisthenics.

That changed in a hurry when Coach gave his next directive. "Every time I blow my whistle, I want you all to drop and give me five push-ups. Then pop up and get right back to the running. Start now." And he blew his whistle.

Donald dropped with the others and managed the five push-ups, feeling the strain all the way from his shoulders down to his fingers.

Why am I doing this? he wondered.

He kept wondering that for fifteen more minutes as they alternated running with push-ups. But when the session finally ended and he looked around at the exhausted wrestlers making their way to the locker room, he couldn't help but feel more than a little bit proud to be one of them.

2

Stepping Up

Everything in the locker room was painted gray: the walls, the floor, even the ·lockers themselves. The only color in the room was a red poster with black lettering that read HUDSON CITY HORNETS. The room was small and was divided in two by a line of lockers in the center. Tradition had it that the eighth-graders were on one side of the wall of lockers and the seventh-graders on the other.

There was laughter and energy on the eighth-grade side of the lockers, but things were quiet over here.

Donald stood in front of his locker in his underwear and wiped his wiry body dry with a towel. Mario was seated on the bench next to him, staring at the floor with his chin in his hands, too tired to move. Everybody, in fact, seemed to be having the same thought: *Is this really going to be worth it?*

Mario leaned toward Donald. "How many times you get pinned?" he asked.

"About a thousand," Donald replied. "Every two or three seconds. It was tons of fun."

Mario shook his head. "Me, too. Did you pin Tavo at all?"

"You kidding? I could barely touch the guy." He reached into his locker and took out his sneakers and pants. "I'll get him, though. I'll show him a thing or two as soon as I figure him out."

"How long you think that'll take?"

"Two days. Maybe three."

Mario laughed. "Or two years."

"We'll see," Donald replied. "I got more going for me than you think."

He could hear Freddy and Tavo and the other eighth-graders joking around and laughing. "They think they're big shots," he whispered to Mario. "They won't be laughing in a few days, believe me. . . . At least Tavo won't."

The November air had a cold bite to it, but it felt great against Donald's flushed face as he walked across the blacktop basketball court outside the gym. The sun was already down, and the street-lights had come on. He turned to Kendrick, who was putting on his jacket as they walked.

"So what'd you think?"

Kendrick let out his breath in a low whistle. "Hard work," he said. "How 'bout you?"

"About a hundred times harder than anything I ever did," Donald replied.

He stopped walking as they reached the street. "Which way are you going?"

"Down to the Boulevard. Over to Eleventh."

Donald was headed in the same direction, but he lived all the way down on Second Street, nearly in Jersey City. They started walking again.

"It was rough," Donald said, "but I didn't let it

get to me. That's the whole point, isn't it?"

"Guess so." Kendrick yawned and rubbed his shoulder. "Man, I'll sleep tonight. Every muscle hurts."

They walked past the post office and the YMCA and reached Eleventh Street, where Kendrick said, "I'm out of here. See you tomorrow in English."

"Looking forward to it. I get *really* excited learning about adverbs and prepositions."

"Me, too."

"Wake me up when it's over."

So Donald continued along the Boulevard alone, stopping in the grocery store at the corner of Ninth for a small carton of orange juice. Tired and hungry as he was, he was in no hurry to get home. His mom had lost her job the month before, so he was pretty sure he'd be having peanut butter for dinner again. He'd already eaten that for lunch.

The Boulevard had never seemed longer. It was thirteen blocks from school to home, and after all that running it felt like ten miles.

How did Manny do it, running four or five miles every day after school and loving every step of it?

He'd turned into a champion cross-country runner this fall, outdistancing older kids to win the league and district titles.

Several of Donald's friends had begun to have real success in athletics now that they'd reached junior high school. Donald had been on plenty of sports teams, too, but he had to admit that the most successful kids worked harder at it than he did. He'd decided to become a wrestler after attending some high-school matches the winter before. It would be great to finally compete against people his own size, unlike the huge linemen he'd had to contend with in football or the giants he'd met up with on the YMCA basketball court.

Pound for pound, Donald knew he was as tough as anybody. But since he weighed only eighty-seven pounds he was at a disadvantage in many sports. Wrestling would be different, but it sure wouldn't be easy.

He set his backpack on a bus-stop bench, putting on a black knit cap and pulling it down over his ears. He sat there for a few minutes and drank his juice, watching the cars and buses and trucks go by on one of the county's busiest streets.

He was exhausted. A shower and an early bedtime would be great, but of course there was that math homework and some reading to do for social studies. He'd never had much homework in elementary school, but the teachers piled it on in seventh grade.

It had been a full year since he'd been on a sports team. Junior football in sixth grade had been his last official season. He'd started to feel left behind as his friends moved on to more advanced athletic programs, especially Manny. They'd been best friends for a long time, but Manny had definitely stepped up. Now it seemed like it was Donald's turn to do the same.

He shot the empty juice carton toward a garbage can, but it struck the rim and fell to the sidewalk. Donald frowned, picked up his backpack, and retrieved the carton.

His mom was waiting at the door when he arrived, and she stepped out to the porch and smiled. They lived on one side of a brick duplex; both sides were the same, only opposite. Donald could smell something cooking, warm and cheesy.

"Hi," she said enthusiastically. "Long day, huh?"

"It was brutal. What smells so good?"

"Macaroni and cheese. I thought you'd want something hot."

"Great. You find a job?"

"Not yet. But your dad's working another double shift, so that's good. He won't be home until midnight."

Mr. Jenkins worked at a factory in Newark. The work was fairly steady, but the family had always struggled to pay the rent and other bills.

Donald's parents were quite a bit older than most of his friends' parents. They hadn't even met until they were in their thirties. Donald had no brothers or sisters.

"Dinner's ready?" he asked.

"It's been ready. I didn't know you'd be so late."

"Neither did I. They worked us just about to death. The coach actually said he was taking it easy on us because it was the first day. I guess tomorrow we'll run a marathon and drag a school bus up a hill."

"I'd better give you a double helping of dinner."

"The day after that we have to swim across the Hudson River wearing metal vests."

"That'll be something to see."

"Yeah, well, we're wrestlers. We're tough."

"So I gather."

He sat at the kitchen table and shut his eyes. The cat appeared and rubbed her head against his shin.

"It wasn't *that* hard, I guess. I'll be sore tomorrow, but I liked it. Most of it, anyway. I hated the running, but when we actually wrestled it was cool. I'm pretty quick; I took a few guys down."

Mom sat across from him, and the cat climbed onto her lap. "Did anyone take you down?"

"Just one guy. Nobody else."

She smiled. "I'm not surprised. You've always been elusive, that's for sure."

"Yeah, I know how to slip out of trouble. I think

I might be pretty good at this. I just gotta learn a few more moves."

Donald climbed into bed early after a shower and homework, leaving the light on for now and staring at the ceiling. Despite the cold weather, he had his window open about six inches so he could hear the traffic sounds a couple of blocks away.

Usually he'd listen to the radio at night, an oddball station out of New York City that played oldies from the fifties and sixties and sometimes even earlier. But tonight he didn't want the distraction.

His right elbow was sore where a bit of skin had rubbed off when he was battling to keep Tavo from pinning him, and his legs felt heavy from the running. But those were good hurts; they were the results of his effort.

Except for a few sleepovers at Manny's, Donald had slept in this room every night of his life. Everything in it was familiar: the trophies on his dresser for being a member of championship teams in Little League baseball and YMCA floor hockey, the framed photo on the wall above his bed of Donald and his father fishing off a pier at the Jersey Shore, the pile of board games collecting dust in the corner of the room—Monopoly, Stratego, Clue.

And then there were those patterns in the ceiling's cracked plaster, especially the large one that was roughly the shape of a fat alligator. And toward the edge, above the window, was the pattern he'd first identified as a dog when he was a toddler. Now it looked more to him like a woodchuck.

All of these things were the same as they'd always been, but one thing seemed different to Donald. The difference was in him, the kid lying in bed thinking. He felt as if he'd crossed a line today, like he'd finally started becoming an athlete.

The second day of practice was certain to be even harder. Donald yawned and turned out the light. The cold breeze from outdoors was steady. He huddled under the covers and fell into the deepest sleep he'd had since he was a baby.

3

Mat Burns

Donald could smell coffee brewing as he brushed his teeth in the morning. That would mean that his dad was up. He had only a few minutes before leaving for school, so he hustled into his clothes and trotted down the stairs.

"Hey, Dad!"

"Darnald!" Dad said with a laugh. "Cutting it close, as usual, I see. Not much time for breakfast."

Mr. Jenkins looked like an older version of his son—very lean with a smirky expression, and straight sandy hair that was cut short. The difference was that Dad's hair was already turning gray and he wore glasses.

Donald opened the refrigerator and set the orange-juice carton on the table. He picked up a cold baked potato from a few nights before and stared at it. "How long to microwave this, you think?"

"Half a minute."

"Good deal. Any of that macaroni and cheese left?"

"Should be."

He was very hungry, and lunch was a long way off.

"Mom says you liked the wrestling?"

"Yeah. Discomfort is a lot of fun."

"Your muscles hurting this morning?"

"Not too bad. I can walk. A little."

Dad rolled his eyes. "Maybe we'd better call a limousine to take you to school. Or a helicopter."

"That'd be great, Dad. Have them pick me up after practice, too."

"That'll really impress your teammates."

"I know it."

Donald wolfed down his food and grabbed his backpack. "Still cold out?"

"Very. Feels like winter already."

"It won't last. You working tonight?"

"I expect to."

"Then I'll see you tomorrow morning."

Dad stood and kissed the top of Donald's head.

"Oh, man!" Donald said. "I forgot to make my lunch."

Dad rolled his eyes and took his wallet from his back pocket. "This'll break the bank, but I guess you'd better buy lunch today." He handed Donald a couple dollars. "Work hard," he said.

"Thanks," Donald said as he stepped out to the porch. "Yeah, work is hard."

Manny was waiting on the Boulevard. He pointed to his wrist to indicate that they were running late. And he swung his backpack gently at Donald. "It's cold, man. I been waiting here for five minutes."

"Poor guy. I'm weeping for you."

"I have math problems to finish in homeroom."

"Should've done 'em last night," Donald said.

"Like you should talk. I watched Monday Night Football instead."

They had to run the last three blocks to avoid being late.

"My legs are beat," Donald said as they hustled up the steps outside the school.

"It's good for you."

"We ran forever yesterday. You probably went out and did fifty miles just for fun."

"Only three. I'm resting this week."

"Doesn't sound like resting to me."

Donald took his seat in his homeroom just seconds before the late bell. He turned to Mario, seated behind him, and noticed a raw spot on his cheek.

"Your face looks like my elbow."

"That's called a mat burn," Mario said. "My brother says to expect a lot of them if we keep wrestling."

"What do you mean *if?*"

"I mean . . . You know what I mean. Expect a lot of sore skin."

"Doesn't scare me."

"Me either," Mario said. "A couple of guys already said they're quitting, though."

"Like who?"

"Ricky said he is. And he said Jordan is out, too. They hated it."

Donald could understand the temptation to quit. You either loved the physical challenge or you didn't. He was pretty sure he loved it. "Hope we get more one-on-one time today," he said. "You know, actually get to wrestle somebody again. Anybody but Tavo, I mean."

"That's how I got this," Mario said, pointing to the mat burn on his face. "But I know what you mean. That's why we went out for this sport in the first place."

"Right. I mean, I *love* doing push-ups until my fingers snap off, but the actual wrestling is even better."

"Yeah," Mario said. "My favorite was running in

place for four hours. I think we were supposed to dig a hole in the mat with our feet."

"That's the idea. Do drills until the gym caves in, then wrestle on the debris."

"That's what makes us tough."

Donald turned to face the front of the room. School days were long, but at least now he had something to look forward to at the end of it.

4

Flat on His Back

Donald squirmed and twisted, but Tavo was just too strong. Why did Coach keep putting Donald against him?

Just like yesterday, Tavo was using Donald as a takedown dummy. He'd pinned him four times already.

I could beat half the guys in this gym, Donald thought. *Is Coach trying to make me look bad or what?*

Donald felt his shoulders pressing firmly into the mat for pin number five.

"Got ya," Tavo said, grabbing Donald's arm and hauling him up.

Donald swatted at Tavo and said, "Knock it off. I told you I don't need any help."

"Just giving you a hand, bro."

Donald made a fist and lifted it up. "You'll get a hand. A clenched one."

Tavo laughed. They were the same size, but obviously he'd have no more trouble handling Donald in a fight than in a wrestling match.

Donald didn't care. He took a step closer and leaned forward with his face just inches from Tavo's. "You'll be dead meat after I learn a few moves," he said.

Tavo leaned forward, too, so his forehead was almost touching Donald's. Donald put a hand on Tavo's chest and shoved hard.

Tavo took a step back, nearly falling to the mat. He reached up and gripped Donald's shirt with one hand, staring at him hard. "Don't get me mad."

"Let go," Donald said. "I'm already mad."

Tavo let go of the shirt and laughed again. That didn't help Donald's anger any.

Donald felt a finger jabbing into his shoulder.

He looked up and saw Coach standing there. "Problem here?"

"No."

"No?"

Donald shook his head.

Coach made the same circling motion with his hand that he'd made the day before. "Start running," he said.

"Just me?"

"Just you. I saw what happened. I don't care how bad you get beat, but if you act like a poor sport you get punished."

Donald let out his breath in a huff and walked to the edge of the mat. Then he started running laps around the gym, much faster than yesterday. He couldn't help but run faster because he was angry. Tavo had made him look like a jerk.

Coach sent word for Tavo and Donald to come to the office after practice. All of the school's sports coaches shared the same office: a tiny, cramped space next to the locker room with a desk, two chairs, and a bulletin board with team schedules and announcements.

Both boys stood outside the office for about ten minutes while Coach talked on the phone. They didn't say anything. Donald glanced at Tavo without turning his head. The guy had bigger arm muscles than he did, and he stood straighter. And he had confidence, no doubt about that.

Coach was apparently talking to his wife. "Look, it'll happen when he's ready. He's just being stubborn. . . . Give him a book to look at. . . . The one with the bird who lost his mother; he's got that one memorized. . . . Well, we can't force him. He'll get it sooner or later."

Finally Coach hung up. "My two-year-old," he said, swiveling in his chair to face the boys. "Toilet training."

Coach looked at Donald. "You learn anything today, Jenkins?"

Donald shrugged. "I suppose."

Coach pointed to Tavo but kept his eyes on Donald. "When you go against a smart wrestler like Tavo, you can't let yourself get frustrated." He pointed to his head. "Clear thinking. If you start seeing red, you'll get pounded. He'll pin you in a second. You've got balance and heart and pretty good strength, and I suspect you've got some brains, too."

Coach stopped talking and gave Donald a hard stare.

"Okay," Donald said.

"You'll turn out to be a good wrestler if you stick with it and control your temper. After Tavo pins you about a hundred more times, I suspect you'll start to catch on."

Donald blushed. He looked sideways at Tavo. Tavo nudged him with his elbow and gave him an upward nod, looking kind of friendly, which was a surprise.

"You may not like it, but wrestling Tavo every day is the best gift a wrestler like you could get," Coach said. "He'll keep slaughtering you, but you'll get better a lot faster than if I paired you with somebody else.

"One more thing: If you start fights, you'll be off the team. Now get out of here." He waved them back toward the lockers.

Donald followed Tavo back. As they reached the locker room, Tavo turned and said, "Guys who lose their temper get eaten alive in this sport."

Donald didn't reply.

Kendrick was dressed and tying his shoes when Donald got back. Most of the other seventh-graders were already gone.

"You in trouble?" Kendrick asked.

"Nah."

"What was with the extra running today?"

"Me and Tavo got in a scruffle. It was no big deal."

"I didn't see *him* running."

Donald yanked his soaking T-shirt over his head and fumbled with his lock. "I guess he was too tired."

"Yeah, right."

They were the last two in the locker room now. Coach came in and chased them out. Donald grabbed his backpack and put on his sneakers without tying them. "See you tomorrow, Coach. I'll be the one flat on my back again."

5

First Match

Two weeks passed quickly, with rugged workouts and constant learning of new wrestling moves. Tavo had continued to pin Donald repeatedly during practice, but Coach demonstrated a few counter moves that helped him fend off a few of the attacks.

The work made Donald hungry all the time. He'd sit in his morning classes wishing the clock would move more quickly so he could eat lunch.

Now here he was, suited up in the red-and-black Hudson City wrestling uniform, nervously stretching and running in place, minutes away from his first real match.

He put on his headgear and fastened the chin-strap, letting out a deep breath and staring at the mat in the center of the Hudson City gym. Mario was out there now, struggling to keep from getting pinned by his faster and more limber opponent.

Coach was loudly instructing Mario what to do—"Roll out of it!"—but the Jersey City wrestler had Mario in a half nelson and was forcing his shoulders toward the mat.

Donald winced as the referee smacked the mat to signal a pin. Mario had only lasted about fifty seconds. Would Donald do any better? He'd soon find out.

Donald's match was one of five preliminaries before the meet would officially begin. He hadn't earned a spot in the starting lineup, but fortunately the other team had several junior varsity wrestlers, too, so he'd be getting a taste of real competition.

Coach gripped Donald's shoulder and told him to stay focused and be patient. "No big heroic moves right off," he said. "Wait for your opening, then be as aggressive as you can. Think on your feet."

Donald glared at his opponent, who looked a little shorter but a bit stronger, more solidly built. His mouth was set in an angry line.

How good could he be? Donald wondered. *He didn't make their varsity.*

And he probably hadn't been training against someone as skilled as Tavo every day, either.

Stop thinking, Donald thought. *Just kick this guy's butt.*

There were only about twenty spectators in the small bleachers, but Manny and a few of Donald's other friends were there.

The referee waved the two wrestlers onto the mat. They shook hands and backed away, staring viciously at each other and waiting for the whistle to start the match.

Two two-minute periods. If it lasted that long.

They circled around each other, testing their quickness with a few false lunges. Then Donald saw an opening: The Jersey City wrestler had his right foot too far forward. Donald dodged toward his opponent's left leg, forcing him to shift his right one even farther up. This gave Donald a perfect shot at that leg, and he took advantage.

Donald made that penetrating first step just as Coach had been stressing all week, keeping his arms close to his body as he attacked. He locked his hands behind his opponent's right knee. From there it was easy to lift him and force him to the mat, and Donald had the lead.

He heard the cheers of his teammates and the spectators, but his focus was completely on working this guy's shoulders toward the mat. But his opponent was resisting, squirming to get out of Donald's grip. He wouldn't be easy to pin.

Donald hung on, but the Jersey City wrestler managed to get to his knees.

"Go for the ankle!" Tavo yelled from the sideline.

Donald knew that would be his best move, lifting the guy's ankle from the mat and forcing him to lie flat. Tavo used that move on Donald all the time.

The trick was to shift his hand from the guy's

waist to his ankle, doing it quickly enough that he couldn't escape.

Don't think, just do it, Donald told himself.

The move worked. The Jersey City wrestler was flat on his stomach with Donald on top, lifting that ankle with one hand and trying to turn the guy with the other.

But Donald didn't quite have the strength to take advantage of the position. The guy simply squirmed toward the edge of the mat, finally rolling them both out of bounds.

So the referee brought them to the center of the mat again. Since Donald had been in control when they went out of bounds, he would maintain his advantage. The Jersey City wrestler kneeled on the mat, hands flat, too, and Donald kneeled behind him, one hand on his opponent's waist and the other at his elbow.

"Flatten this guy!" came a call from the crowd. Donald was sure it came from Manny.

The whistle blew and both wrestlers worked furiously—Donald trying to force his opponent down again and the opponent trying to escape. Donald felt his grip loosening; the guy had broken free. In an instant they were both on their feet again, circling around as before.

But Donald had earned the best of that exchange. His takedown was worth two points, while the Jersey City wrestler's escape was worth just one.

Plenty of time remained in the period. Donald wanted another takedown. What he really wanted was a pin.

His opponent apparently hadn't learned anything from that first takedown; he still had his right leg too far forward, almost inviting Donald to attack. So Donald feinted toward the left leg again, then shot over to the right and quickly executed the takedown.

He's dead meat now, Donald thought, working to turn the takedown into a pinning combination. But the guy got to one knee and forced himself up, escaping just as quickly as Donald had taken him down.

Now Donald had a 4–2 lead, and time was winding down to the end of the first period. Donald was clearly the more aggressive athlete. The Jersey City wrestler seemed content just to play defense.

Donald knew enough to take advantage of that. He went right back at the guy, penetrating low and reaching for both legs this time.

But his opponent was ready. He stepped straight back, and Donald crashed to the mat, facedown with his hands clutching nothing but air. The Jersey City wrestler deftly scurried across, and in an instant he had Donald in the same half-nelson grip that Mario's opponent had used.

With no momentum and no leverage, Donald was helpless to keep from being turned to his back. He struggled desperately to keep his shoulders up, but the guy was just too strong.

Wham. The referee slapped the mat, signaling a pin.

Donald was stunned. Seconds before, he'd had the match under his control. And just like that, because of one poorly executed move, he'd lost.

He barely looked at the referee or his opponent as they shook hands again, then walked dejectedly off the mat. Coach slapped him on the shoulder and said, "Good effort," but he immediately turned his attention to the next match.

Donald slumped in a folding chair next to Mario and stared at his feet. "I was killing that guy," he muttered. "He got *so* lucky. I can't believe it."

6

Time to Unwind

Hudson City won the match, but that didn't do much to lift Donald's spirits. He quickly changed clothes in the locker room while his teammates celebrated, leaving his sweatshirt hood up and not even bothering to tie his sneakers.

He slammed his locker shut and looked around. Steam from the showers was floating overhead, and he could hear Freddy and Tavo and the other eighth-graders laughing and bragging about their wins on the other side of the lockers.

"I'm out of here," he said to Kendrick, who didn't look any happier than Donald. "See you tomorrow."

"Yeah," Kendrick said flatly. Kendrick had made it to the second period of his match, but eventually he'd been pinned, too. "I'll be here."

Donald put his knapsack over one shoulder and stepped outside. He nodded to Manny, who was sitting on the blacktop with his back to the gymnasium wall.

"Thought you'd be a while longer than that," Manny said.

"I just wanted to get out of there as fast as I could."

"You tired from the match?"

"No way." Donald wiped his nose with the sleeve of his sweatshirt. "I've got so much energy I don't know what to do with it. I mean, we've been practicing for *two hours* a day for weeks. Today was like, what? A minute and a half? I hardly felt it."

Manny grinned slyly as he got to his feet. "A minute and a half of work used to be more than you could handle. All of a sudden you're wanting more?"

Donald shrugged. "Mostly I'm mad, I guess. I

had that guy nailed. No *way* he should have beat me."

"You'll get 'em next time."

"I feel like I should do a thousand push-ups or sprint ten miles."

Manny started walking, turning his head to face Donald. "Okay, then here's the plan," he said. "Eight o'clock I'm running three hard miles, then a few sprints. From there I'm meeting a couple of guys at Villa Roma for pizza. If you want to join me for either activity, or both, I'll be glad to have you along."

"Kind of dark for running."

"I'm going to the track. The lights are on until nine."

Donald rolled his eyes and looked up at the dark sky. The clouds were moving quickly in a stiff wind. "All right," he said, letting out his breath in a mist. "I won't be able to keep up with you, but I'll give it a shot."

"Wear gloves," Manny said. "And bring some money."

* * *

"Good news," said Donald's mom as she placed a roasted chicken on the kitchen table. "I got a temporary job at the Kmart in Jersey City. Just until Christmas, but it'll help."

"We'll be back to eating sirloin steak in no time," Dad said.

"Like we ever eat steak anyway," Donald said.

"Right. But this chicken sure beats hot dogs, huh?"

Donald reached for the salt and pepper shakers, which were shaped and painted to look like mermaids. "Okay if I hang out with Manny for a while tonight?" he asked.

"Do you have your homework done?" Mom asked.

"No, but I don't have much. I'll do it right after we eat."

"Are you going to his house?"

"Nah. We're going to Villa Roma, okay?"

"You're going to eat again?"

Donald shrugged. "I'll probably just have a

soda or something. Maybe one slice of pizza. But I haven't been out in weeks. It's been nothing but wrestling."

"Yeah," Dad said. "You need to unwind. You've been wrestling and I've been working double shifts. I don't think we've all had dinner together in two weeks."

"Well," Mom said, shaking her head with a smile, "better enjoy it while you can. I'll be working until nine most nights for the next month."

"We won't even recognize each other by Christmas," Dad said with a laugh. "Darnald will be huge by then, with all that working out and pizza."

"We're going to jog some before the pizza."

Dad raised his eyebrows. "That doesn't sound like resting to me."

"It'll be all right. I've got energy to burn. I'm still keyed up from the match."

"Sorry we missed it."

"You didn't miss much."

7

Pigging Out

Donald had never run farther than a mile in his life—they made 'em do that in gym class once a year—but he figured he wouldn't have much trouble running two. Maybe if Manny took it easy for a few laps Donald could stay with him, but he knew his friend would be way ahead once he started pushing.

Manny was no bigger than Donald, but he was fast and determined and seemed to be able to run all day. That was his sport. Donald was going to make wrestling his own.

"You gotta relax and work into it," Manny said as they began running their first lap at the Hudson

City High School track. The wind was directly in their faces as they started, but both boys were in full sweat suits, with knitted caps and gloves.

Two large lights were on above the bleachers, but it never quite got dark anywhere in Hudson City anyway. There were streetlights on every corner and lots of traffic, plus the glow from New York City just down the hill and across the wide river.

Donald was breathing hard as they rounded the second turn, but Manny seemed effortless. He kept chatting and coaching—"Let your arms swing in a nice rhythm. Nothing should be tense."—but Donald just grunted and kept working. It was obvious to him that Manny was holding back, running slowly to stay with Donald.

"You can go ahead," Donald said as they finished the first lap.

"I'll stick with you for a mile," Manny said. "I always do an easy warm-up."

But after three laps Manny started to accelerate, and by the time Donald had finished six laps, Manny had done seven. Donald struggled through two more to make it an even two miles, then leaned against the fence and watched his friend hammer out a few more laps.

"Felt good," Manny said as he walked over to Donald. "First time I've really let loose since cross-country season."

"Had enough?"

"Not quite. I've got an indoor meet coming up. I need to do some strides."

So Donald watched while Manny did a few quick 100-meter runs.

"Time to eat," Manny said, motioning with his arm for Donald to join him as he walked toward the opening in the fence.

"Didn't you have supper?"

"A little. But I can pig out now. Let's go."

They walked along the rutted sidewalk down Sixth Street, past tight rows of houses, until they reached the Boulevard.

"Who we meeting?" Donald asked.

"Anthony. Maybe Calvin."

Donald and Manny had been best friends since

they were little, but Manny's circle had grown larger because of the track-and-field team. Donald had been jealous of that at first.

They reached Villa Roma, which was crowded with high-school kids. A television above the pizza counter was tuned to a music-video station, and the other one in the opposite corner was showing a college basketball game. But both sets were drowned out by the jukebox, which was playing an old Rolling Stones song. The place smelled warm and toasty from the pizzas baking in the large ovens.

Donald spotted Anthony and Calvin in the corner near the video games.

"You guys order a pie?" Manny said.

"Yep," said Anthony, getting Manny in a gentle headlock. Anthony Martin was probably the biggest guy in seventh grade—a football lineman and a shot-putter on the track team. Calvin Tait also played football and ran track. He and Manny often teamed up on relays.

"Spotted any girls?" Calvin asked.

"None our age," Donald said. "Mostly high-school people in here tonight."

"Yeah, they took all the tables," Anthony said. "We'll have to sit on the floor to eat."

"No problem," Donald said. He leaned against the wall, hands in the big front pocket of his sweat-shirt, which said GIANTS.

Anthony went up to the counter and brought back the pizza, which he set on top of the video game. He grabbed a slice and took a seat on the floor next to Calvin, their backs against the wall.

Donald picked up a slice and took a huge bite.

"Don't you wrestlers have to watch your weight?" Calvin asked.

"I'd like to watch it go *up*," Donald replied. "I could gain three pounds and still be in the same weight class. Mostly it's the bigger guys who want to cut."

He had been thinking about trying to gain a bit of weight. Tavo was a lock to stay in the 90-pound weight class, so there wasn't much chance Donald would be wresting varsity unless he moved up in weight. Donald had wrestled the 95-pounder, Jesse Nadel, in practice a few times. Despite the disadvantage in weight, Donald was more competitive with Jesse than with Tavo.

Donald took a second slice of pizza and slid to a seated position on the floor between Anthony and Calvin. He kept his eyes on the door, watching who went in and out. A lot of the athletes hung out here, so he wasn't too surprised when he saw Hector Mateo walk in. Hector was a senior and the standout on the high-school wrestling team. Watching him compete the year before, in fact, had been a big part of Donald's inspiration to try the sport.

What did surprise Donald was who Hector was with: Tavo. Hector was four years older than Tavo. Why would he be hanging out with him?

Donald watched as Hector and Tavo joined a group of high-school guys at one of the tables. Hector took off his letterman's jacket. Underneath he was wearing a blue soccer jersey that said PUERTO RICO. He had a thin chain around his neck, and his short hair was freshly styled.

Donald felt a little uneasy. He and Tavo hadn't had any run-ins since Donald had shoved him that day at practice, but they'd never quite resolved things, either. Tavo seemed very easygoing, but you never knew what might happen off school grounds.

So Donald tensed a little when Tavo caught his eye and started walking over. He was dressed pretty well, and his hair was styled like Hector's.

"Jenkins," Tavo said, nodding as he looked down at Donald.

"Rivera," Donald replied.

"What's up, Martin?" Tavo said, gripping Anthony's hand and pumping it.

Donald stood up. Tavo sent him to the floor so often in practice that he figured he didn't need to be there now.

"You wrestled pretty much all right today," Tavo said. "The inexperience got to you, though."

"I shoulda won anyway. The guy just got lucky. It was probably his first match, too."

"No." Tavo shook his head, keeping his eyes locked on Donald's. "I was at wrestling camp with that kid last summer. He's in eighth."

"Really?"

"Yeah. He's not a bad wrestler." A smile crossed Tavo's face. "He's smart."

Donald felt himself blush. "I'm smart."

"Smart but dumb. What I mean is, you're smart enough to learn. But nobody can know what they don't know yet, you know what I mean?"

"Sort of."

"Good wrestlers make their own luck," Tavo said. "They know how to finish the job."

Donald jutted his chin toward Hector. "What are you doing hanging out with him?"

"We're just picking up some pizza and wings for home," Tavo said. "He's my brother. Half-brother, anyway."

"Oh. He teach you much?"

"All the time. He knows every move in the book."

"Yeah, I've seen him wrestle."

"Gonna win the state this winter," Tavo said.

"I don't doubt it."

Tavo turned to Calvin and started talking about tennis, which Donald had absolutely no interest in. So he slumped back to the floor and listened to the music. There was almost nothing current on the jukebox, just classic rock and things like Sinatra and Johnny Cash, plus some Latin American stuff, since nearly half the people in Hudson City were Cuban or Puerto Rican or Dominican or Mexican.

Everybody liked pizza, though.

Hector had two pizza boxes in his arms, and he caught Tavo's eye and jerked his head toward the door.

"See you guys later," Tavo said. He pointed at Donald. "Coach said tomorrow we'll show you how to get out of that half nelson."

"Sounds good."

"Don't eat too much. You'll get fat."

"I wish."

Manny took a seat on the floor next to Donald. "You wrestle him a lot?"

"He kicks my butt every single day. Every time I think I'm ready to turn the tide he throws some new move at me." Donald shrugged his shoulders very slowly and gave a half smile. "The guy's good, I gotta admit that."

"Well," Manny said, "the only reason I got good in track was because I got to compete against the best guys around. First time I ran in New York, it was like, whoa, these guys are *quick.* But when I finally started to realize that I could keep up with them, it gave me a whole new boost of confidence."

"Yeah. I guess I'd feel the same if I could beat Tavo just once. I haven't even come close yet."

"And beating him is the only way to get on varsity?"

"That's how it works," Donald said. "You wrestle junior varsity unless you can knock off the varsity guy in your weight class. Coach says we'll have wrestle-offs the day before every match. If a guy like me challenges Tavo in the wrestle-off, then he has to beat me to keep his spot on varsity. If

I beat him, then he drops down to JV."

"That's fair. The top guy has to prove himself every time to keep his spot."

"Right. But when you've got somebody like Tavo in your class, it makes it impossible for me or Mario to move up."

Manny shook his head. "Not impossible."

"Pretty close."

"Maybe you need to try a different weight class."

Donald stared at the pizza crust in his hand for a few seconds. "We're in the lightest class already. Anyway, you're allowed to wrestle in a heavier class, but not a lighter one. So, yeah, I could challenge somebody heavier, but I'm already only eighty-seven pounds. If I went after the guy at ninety-five or a hundred it'd be a big disadvantage."

"You never know. You're already at a disadvantage against Tavo."

Donald nodded slowly, then shoved the pizza crust into his mouth. He chewed carefully—the crust was his favorite part—then swallowed.

Manny might have something there. Maybe there was more than one path to varsity.

A freezing rain was falling by the time Donald crawled into bed that night, but he kept his window open a crack anyway. He loved to huddle nice and warm under all those covers but still feel a breath of cold air on top of his head.

His radio was on softly, tuned to his favorite station, the eccentric one out of New York City. The whole house was dark. Donald heard his door being pushed open, then a soft thud as the cat landed at his feet on the bed. She settled down within seconds and went to sleep.

Some woman named Etta James was singing a jazzy, kick-butt song called "Tell Mama." That was followed by Bob Dylan doing "When the Ship Comes In." Donald had heard that one before; it was already on the list of songs he wanted to remember. Next came something slow and twangy called "Tecumseh Valley."

Donald turned on his light and took a small

notebook out of the drawer of his bedside table. He added the names of those songs and the people who sang them to his list, waiting for the last one to finish and the announcer to name the artist: Townes Van Zandt. Donald put an asterisk next to that one. The list was growing pretty long and included all kinds of music—rock, folk, jazz, old-time country.

It was more than the music that excited Donald, though. The words of those songs were powerful.

It was late and he was tired, and he had school and practice again tomorrow. But he had begun to really savor this time each evening, just relaxing beneath his warm covers with the breeze coming in and the radio on. This felt like a reward after all that hard work he'd been doing. It was his time to think, or just to listen. It amazed him how writers could capture so much emotion and insight in just a few lines of a song.

Suddenly he knew what he wanted for Christmas. A guitar.

He shut off the light and turned to his side, giving the cat a gentle shove. He gripped his forearm. The muscle there was harder than it used to be and maybe a bit bigger. His shoulders were a little tight, the result of fighting a losing battle to keep from getting pinned that afternoon. But they'd be okay. He could take it. That loss still stung, but he knew he'd get better.

He soon drifted off to sleep with the radio on.

8

Half Nelsons

"**W**ork your way out of it!" Coach shouted. "Think about what he's doing to you."

Donald squirmed and strained, but Tavo easily forced his shoulders to the mat for a pin. It was the same move the Jersey City wrestler had used to pin him the day before.

A few feet away, Mario was being pinned via that same half-nelson move by Jesse Nadel.

"The half nelson is the most likely pinning move you're going to be up against," Coach said. "Both of you guys"—he pointed to Mario, then Donald—"lost that way yesterday. So let's work on some counter moves. Learn how to get out of it."

Coach had Jesse get Tavo in the half nelson. "Like this," he said. "Let's say Jesse has just taken Tavo down. So Tavo's on his side, with his arms out."

Jesse hooked his left arm under Tavo's left, then gripped the back of Tavo's head with it. From there he had plenty of leverage to force Tavo over and toward the mat.

"Now, what should Tavo do to counter that?" Coach asked Donald.

Donald shrugged. "Push back as hard as he can?"

"Yeah, but how? Go ahead, Tavo."

Tavo dug his left elbow into the mat to stop Jesse's thrust, then turned his head away, reducing Jesse's leverage. With his left hand, Tavo reached up and forced Jesse's hand off the back of his neck. Now that Jesse had lost the advantage, Tavo was able to spin free and quickly get to his feet.

"Perfect," Coach said. "There are other ways out, but let's work on this one. Pair up again and let's go."

So Donald went to the mat and let Tavo apply the hold.

"Like Tavo needs for me to *let* him put a half nelson on me?" Donald remarked. "He does it in about two seconds even when I start out on my feet."

Coach laughed. "So let's not waste the two seconds. Let's go."

Tavo applied the grip, and Donald got his elbow down. Tavo's hand began to slip from Donald's neck, but then it got tighter. Tavo was strong. He managed to turn Donald over anyway.

"Try it again," Coach said. "You're at a big disadvantage, Jenkins, because Tavo knows exactly what you're trying to do. In a match things happen much more quickly. It becomes almost automatic if you work on it enough."

They went through the drill several more times. Donald never quite managed to get out of the grip, but he lengthened the time it took Tavo to pin him. And when they switched partners, with Tavo taking on Mario and Donald matched up with Jesse, things changed in a hurry.

Jesse was a few pounds heavier than Donald— he was the first-string wrestler at ninety-five pounds—but it was clear that he didn't have Tavo's strength or flexibility. Donald got out of the grip twice. And when it was his turn to put the half nelson on Jesse, he came very close to executing a pin.

That was the breakthrough he was looking for. The rest of the practice session—crunches, leg lifts, running in place—was just as tough as ever, but it had taken on a new meaning for Donald. He was making progress. All this work was paying off.

He showered and dressed, then sat in front of his locker and rubbed a sore spot above his knee. Mario sat next to him on the bench.

"Tavo is like a cross between a cougar and a machine or something," Mario said with frustration. "The guy is so strong and flexible. I don't envy you having to go against *him* every day."

"Yeah, he's a monster," Donald said. He lowered his head and turned to Mario, waving him closer with a finger. "I think I could beat Jesse, though. I think I could take his spot away."

Mario shrugged. "You might. He's definitely not as good as Tavo."

Donald looked around. Most of the wrestlers had left, but he didn't want anybody hearing this. "Just between you and me, I'm gonna ask Coach to let me challenge him for the ninety-five-pound spot."

"You got nothing to lose," Mario said. "Might as well go after it."

"I'm going to. So what if I lose? I'll just challenge him again until I beat him."

"Sounds like a plan," Mario said. "You never know—if you get on varsity then I might wind up challenging *you* in a few weeks."

"That's all right with me. We keep knocking each other off, and sooner or later we'll actually get good at this sport."

9

No Escape

Donald hustled down the hallway toward his math class, running late as usual. The hallways were mostly empty; he had spent too many minutes talking to Kendrick after English class, and the late bell was about to ring.

"Slow down, buddy," came a familiar voice. Donald looked up to see Coach Mills walking toward him. Coach taught eighth-grade science.

Donald shook his head. "Mrs. Epstein said I'd get detention if I was late again."

"Slow down anyway. I'll write you a pass."

"That'd be cool." Donald stopped and leaned

against a locker, looking up at his coach. "If I got detention I'd be late for practice."

"Wouldn't want to let that happen. Especially now that you're on a roll."

"Yeah, I'm getting the hang of it, I think."

"You'll be good," Coach said. "It just takes time."

Donald nodded. "I been wanting to ask you something. I'm not going to be beating Tavo any-time soon, but do you think I could wrestle-off with Jesse at ninety-five?"

Coach squinted and gave Donald a good looking-over. "I hadn't really thought about it. I'm not sure if you're ready."

"But that's how you find out, isn't it? If he beats me, so what?"

"Right. You'd probably give him a good match. But what I'm thinking is that you might be better off if you get another JV match or two under your belt. Then try for varsity."

Donald puffed out his lips and blew out his

breath. He stood up straighter. "I think I could take Jesse right now."

"You may be right. But look, we've got Bayonne at the end of the week. Great program over there. Even if you did wrestle varsity against them, you'd probably get pounded. Jesse has a lot more experience. I'd rather you go against a more even opponent for at least one more match."

"And then I can challenge Jesse?"

"Probably."

The late bell had already rung. Coach took out a pass and quickly filled it out. "Now you made *me* late," he said. "Maybe you can write me a pass."

Donald laughed and took off down the hall.

Fair enough. He'd wrestle another JV match. But his sights were set squarely on Jesse for next week.

The bus ride to Bayonne was short, but Donald could barely stay seated anyway. He was loaded with energy, eager to get on that mat and demonstrate

how much he'd advanced since that loss against
Jersey City. It had only been a week, but that week
had dragged on forever. He needed to prove to himself that he could win.

"You all right?" Mario asked, staring at him
from the next seat over. Donald was pounding on
his thighs with his fists, letting out his breath in
short, angry bursts.

"Yeah. I'm fine. Just totally fired up. Can't wait
to get out on that mat."

"Save some energy."

"I got plenty."

The bus pulled into the parking lot and Donald
kneeled on the seat, waiting for the wrestlers in
front of him to get into the aisle.

"Let's move it!" he said.

Freddy looked back and gave him a friendly
sneer. "Wait your turn."

"I been waiting all week. I need to *wrestle*."

Freddy and Tavo led the team through a warm-
up, then the varsity wrestlers took seats on the

bottom row of the bleachers. Coach gathered the JV kids near the mat.

"They've got a full team, so all of you will wrestle in the preliminaries," he said. "Mario and Donald— they've got two JV ninety-pounders. Which one of you wants to go first?"

Donald put up his hand. "I'm jumping out of my skin. I gotta get out there."

"All right. But get hold of yourself. You need to be aggressive, but not nuts about it. Remember what happened last time."

"Remember what?" Donald grinned. "Don't worry. It's still right here," he said, pointing to his head.

The Bayonne wrestler was taller and thinner than Donald, but his long arms might be tough to deal with. Donald gave him a good hard stare as they shook hands.

Wrong place, wrong time for you, Donald thought as he waited for the referee's whistle. *Nobody beats me today.*

But eager as he was for a quick attack, Donald found it hard to find an opening in the early going. They circled around each other and made a few false lunges, but neither could gain an advantage. Both were crouched low at the same level.

Suddenly Donald stood up straighter, a simple move he'd seen Tavo do a lot. The Bayonne wrestler mirrored him, and Donald shot low and penetrated, one arm circling his opponent's waist and the other locking behind his opposite knee.

The guy leaned forward into Donald in an attempt to keep his balance, but Donald instinctively turned him and drove forward, bringing his opponent to the mat.

Pin him, Donald thought. *Finish this thing right now.*

But the Bayonne wrestler knew what he was doing and managed to roll to his stomach. Donald definitely had the advantage, but did he have enough strength to finish?

There was lots of time left in the period, but

every move Donald tried was countered by his opponent. Even so, Donald had the lead. He could ride this guy for the rest of the match and be the winner. Both wrestlers were working hard. One or the other would wear down first.

Between periods Coach told Donald to keep applying pressure and try to work that ride into a pinning combination. "You're in control," he said. "You'll start the period on top, and he'll be super aggressive trying to get out of it. Try to break him down and get him on his stomach. Make him carry your weight."

The Bayonne wrestler got down in the starting position, knees and hands on the mat but his head up high. Donald was behind him, hands at his opponent's waist and elbow.

And back they went to the same struggle they had waged during most of the first period. Donald was in control, but each wrestler was working furiously to overpower the other.

The Bayonne wrestler nearly got to his feet a

couple of times, but Donald kept his arms around the guy's waist and his hands locked on his wrists. Both times he managed to bring the guy back to the mat.

So Donald still had a 2–0 lead midway through the period, but he'd never worked harder in his life. Both wrestlers were getting slippery with sweat, and both were straining with the effort.

Finally the Bayonne wrestler got to his feet, and with a violent thrust of his hands he unlocked Donald's grip and wriggled free.

Donald stepped back and let out his held breath. The escape was worth one point; Donald still had the lead.

Okay, now we really see what you're made of, Donald told himself. *Take this guy down again and finish him off.*

"Twenty seconds!" called Coach.

Donald knew he had this match won now. Another takedown would be sweet, but all he really had to do was stay on his feet as the seconds ticked away.

But the Bayonne wrestler knew that he had to have more points, and he needed them quickly. He shot toward Donald and they locked arms, with their hands gripping each other's elbows. Quickly the Bayonne wrestler dropped to his knees, grasping both of Donald's legs.

Donald leaned forward, hands on his opponent's back. And suddenly he felt that sickening feeling he'd known so many times in practice: He was being lifted from the mat. The Bayonne wrestler hooked his right knee around Donald's left. There was no place to go but down.

No! Donald thought. But it was too late. He'd been taken down. He had a few seconds left to get free, to at least tie the score. But his opponent was in control and Donald could not escape. The whistle blew. Donald had lost the match, 3–2.

Again? Donald thought. *I blew it again?*

He stomped off the mat and sat down hard on the Hudson City bench, head in his hands. He tore off the headgear and flung it aside. His head was pounding, and his breath was rapid and shallow.

"Get a grip," Coach said, putting his hand on top of Donald's head. "Watch your temper."

Donald nodded but continued to stare at the floor. After a minute he got up and walked to the locker room, where he leaned against a sink and looked into the mirror.

His face was red, and his hair was soaked with sweat. The expression on his face was sour. He spit into the sink and smacked his forehead with his palm.

"You're a loser," he mumbled. "You had that man beat. You gave it away."

The locker-room door opened, and Tavo came in. He stepped over to the sink next to Donald and fixed his hair with his hands. "You had him," he said.

"No kidding," Donald said sharply. "Listen, man, I'm in no mood. Save the criticism for somebody else."

"No criticism," Tavo said. "I just came in to use the bathroom." He smirked at Donald. "Losing stinks, huh?"

"You got that right."

Tavo smiled and drummed on the sink with his fingers. "You gotta learn how to finish," he said. "You could have pinned that guy fifteen different ways. You just don't know how to do it yet."

"I shoulda won anyway. The guy had nothing."

"He had enough to beat you."

Donald frowned and left the locker room. He looked toward the mat. Mario was walking off with his hands raised and a big smile. The Hudson City wrestlers were whooping it up and clapping.

Guess I should have gone second, Donald thought.

He took a seat by the other wrestlers in the bleachers but said almost nothing the rest of the afternoon. Tavo, Jesse, and Freddy won their matches, but Bayonne managed to win overall.

Would he ever win a match? Twice he'd had

the lead now, and twice he'd managed to lose. It was enough to make a guy want to quit. Even Mario and Jesse had won their matches today.

Maybe this isn't *my sport,* Donald thought as he stared out the bus window on the way back to Hudson City. *Maybe I'm not as tough as I thought I was.*

10

Jealousy

"You heading home?" Kendrick asked after they'd returned to Hudson City.

"Where else would I go?" Donald said.

"I mean, you want to head out together?"

Donald yanked his jacket out of his backpack and shrugged. "Sure."

Kendrick had lost again, too, so they wouldn't be joking around like other days. Donald just wanted to get off the bus in a hurry. He was mad at everybody—at the guy who had beat him, at Tavo for trying to help, even at Mario for winning his own match.

They stepped outside. The air was still and cool.

"The thing that makes me maddest is that I would have beat the guy Mario wrestled," he said.

"So?"

"So now Mario looks like a better wrestler than I am. He won."

"That ain't Mario's fault."

"No. It's mine."

"You might not have beat that other guy."

"I can beat Mario. I would have clobbered his opponent."

"That's not the point. You wrestle who you wrestle. One on one."

They walked along the Boulevard in silence for a few minutes. When they reached the YMCA, Donald stopped. "I'm gonna go in here for a little while," he said.

"How come?"

"I don't know. Just to chill out."

"All right." Kendrick turned and looked up the street. "I need to get home."

"See you tomorrow then. And listen, don't say nothing to Mario. I'm not mad at him. Just jealous, I guess. And mad at myself."

"Sure. I hear you."

The Y was quiet this early in the evening. Donald had spent a lot of time here, but mostly on rowdy Saturdays when he was younger, participating in indoor soccer and floor hockey and basketball leagues. He'd always done all right. Never a star, but usually a pretty good player.

He wasn't sure why he'd come here tonight. Probably because this was one of the few places where he'd ever had much success as an athlete. He needed to be reminded of that.

He walked into the empty gym and set his backpack on the first row of the bleachers. A basketball was lying on the side of the court, and he picked it up and dribbled it a few times.

He spent a few minutes shooting baskets, missing the first several but then getting into a groove and making four in a row. There'd been one game a couple of years ago—a tournament semifinal—

when he'd tossed in a three-pointer in the final minute, then stole a pass and went the length of the court for a game-winning layup.

There hadn't been many moments like that in his sports career, but there'd been one or two others. A fumble recovery that he returned for a touchdown. A bases-clearing triple.

He rolled the basketball to the far end of the court and went downstairs to the weight room.

Three high-school guys were in one corner working on the bench press, and a woman was running on a treadmill. Donald had passed through the weight room a few times, but he'd never lifted weights. Other guys on the wrestling team lifted, and Coach had said that the seventh-graders ought to start doing so in the off-season.

He climbed onto an exercise bike and pedaled slowly for a few minutes, watching the high-school guys lift. They were laughing and busting each other. Loud rock music was blaring from the radio.

How could I lose like that again? he wondered.

He'd felt so ready, so psyched up, so certain that he'd win. Now he felt just the opposite, unsure if he would ever hold on and win one.

His parents were both working tonight, so there was no rush to get home. He had no appetite anyway. He pedaled the bike for ten more minutes, then grabbed his stuff and headed out.

There was still a lot of traffic on the Boulevard, and the restaurants and small grocery stores were open. Donald trudged past, suddenly eager to get home and out of the cold.

After a couple of blocks he heard a horn beeping. He turned and saw his father's car.

"What are you doing out so late?" Dad said as Donald got in.

"Just getting home from the match."

"Must have been a long one."

"It was away. Over in Bayonne."

"You win?"

Donald shook his head. "I should have. I had the guy beat the whole match. I just couldn't finish. Couldn't hold on at the end."

"Tough break."

Mr. Jenkins had never been involved in sports as a kid, but he came to see Donald's events when he had time. He was usually working when the games were scheduled, so it meant a lot to Donald when he got there.

"Are you still having fun with it?" Dad asked.

"I guess. It's not exactly *fun*, you know, like being in Little League or something. It's more like . . . I don't know. It's something I like to do because it makes me push myself."

"I can see that."

"Even when I get my butt kicked, I can feel that I'm getting somewhere. Like sooner or later, if I work hard enough, I'll really start to enjoy it. Just not quite yet."

"Makes sense."

"Nah, it doesn't," Donald said, his temper starting to heat up again. "I mean, I've been working my butt off. I'm tired of being *patient*. I should be winning matches."

They'd reached the house. Dad turned off the

engine, and they sat in the car for a minute. "So, when's the next one?" Dad asked.

"Tuesday. Five more days. We wrestle Palisades at home."

"I'll see if I can get there."

"That would be great if you could."

Donald stared through the windshield at the house. "It's so frustrating," he finally said.

"So why do it?"

"I don't know. To prove something, I guess. That I *can* do it. That I can beat anybody out there. Anybody my size, at least."

"Who do you have to prove that to?" Dad asked. "I mean, I know that's a valuable thing, but you need to figure out why it's important to you."

Donald nodded. "Right. Maybe I don't even know why I do it. I just know that I hate losing. And so far I've done nothing *but* lose."

They both thought that over for a minute. Then Dad gave Donald a soft whack on the knee. "You all right?" he asked.

"I'll get over it. Maybe by tomorrow. We'll see."

He turned to his father and slowly shook his head. "I *will* start winning. I don't know when, but I will."

"No doubt about it," Dad said. "You work hard enough, sooner or later you succeed."

Donald just nodded, but right away he felt better.

"We'd better get in and feed the cat," Dad said.

"Better feed me, too. I'm starving."

11

Double Challenge

Monday was wrestle-off day, when any junior varsity wrestler could challenge a varsity member for his spot in the starting lineup. Donald had made it clear that he was after Jesse's berth at ninety-five pounds.

"We've got two challengers at that weight class," Coach said as the wrestlers took seats in the bleachers. "So, they'll wrestle first to determine who takes on Jesse."

Donald looked around. Mario hadn't said a word, but obviously he was the second challenger. Mario looked at Donald and nodded with a tight smile. Donald made a fist but smiled back.

"Mario and Donald, get out here. After your match, we'll run through the challenges in the other weight classes, then whoever wins your match can go against Jesse."

Donald stepped to the mat and reached for his toes, feeling the stretch in the backs of his legs. So one win wouldn't be enough to get him a spot on varsity. He'd have to beat two guys in a row.

I can handle that, he thought.

He'd spent the entire school day preparing mentally for this match, thinking he'd be going against Jesse. Now he needed to turn that energy toward Mario and keep it going after that.

Maybe he could just pin Mario in a hurry and forget that this match even happened. Then he could get right back to his preparation for Jesse.

But he knew it wouldn't be that easy.

Coach blew his whistle, and Donald and Mario darted about, lunging at each other and then backing away.

Donald managed a takedown halfway through

the period, but Mario twisted out of it and escaped. Then he took Donald down, but Donald made a reversal and retook the lead.

The wrestlers in the bleachers were yelling encouragement as the furious action continued. By the end of the period, Mario had escaped again and Donald had scored another takedown. He had a 6–4 lead, but he was tired.

This is right where he'd been in his previous matches—slightly ahead against a tough opponent. *If I waste this chance, I'm nothing.*

The second period went back and forth, but Donald maintained the lead. Mario escaped; Donald took him down. Mario escaped again. Donald couldn't pin him and couldn't control him for very long, but his quickness was working to his advantage.

Time ran out with Mario desperately trying for a takedown. Donald raised his arms and shut his eyes in triumph.

He'd made the first step. One more to go.

"Nice job," Mario said as they walked off the mat together.

"You, too," Donald said, breathing hard.

They sat together in the bleachers as two other JV guys lost their challenge matches. Next up was Donald against Jesse.

"You can do this," Mario said.

"You didn't help me much." But Donald grinned. "Maybe you did. I'm tired, but I'm good and warmed up. The nerves are gone, too."

"Glad to be of service," Mario said. "By the way, I'm not done yet. You can expect another challenge next week."

"Yeah, but maybe it'll be Jesse and you in the first match next time, vying to try to knock me off. It's like playing King of the Hill."

"Go out there and beat the king then. He's waiting."

Jesse glared at Donald from across the mat. Nobody liked to be challenged, and it was even worse for an eighth-grader to be challenged by someone in seventh. Donald was aware of that, and he did have respect for Jesse. But this was the way wrestling went. The best guy had to prove it every time.

The match was similar to the one against Mario, as both wrestlers were quick and agile but not very skilled at pinning. Jesse scored the first takedown, but Donald quickly reversed him and Jesse quickly escaped.

As Donald expected, he was pretty evenly matched with Jesse. The outcome could go either way. But Donald was getting worn out as the second period wound down. It was his fourth period of wrestling—Jesse had more fuel left.

So it was no surprise that Jesse hung on for a 7–5 win. He gripped Donald's shoulder as they walked off the mat. "Nice match," he said, obviously relieved to have survived.

"Thanks. Way to go."

This loss didn't sting like the others. Donald had wrestled a good match, but his fatigue might have cost him the win. Making varsity probably wasn't too far off. He definitely had his confidence back. And tomorrow he'd be competing again. Another chance to win.

"That's it for today," Coach said. "Get a good meal tonight and a good rest. Palisades is a very talented team. Let's be miserable hosts and beat them."

Donald's parents were still at work when he got home, and he didn't feel like being alone. Too much to think about, with the match tomorrow and all. He picked up the phone and dialed.

"Manny."

"Yeah?"

"You want to come over? Watch TV or something?"

"Let me check."

Donald stroked the cat's back as he waited. His mom had left him a plate of ham and pasta to heat up, but he hadn't eaten it yet. It didn't look very appealing.

"I can stay till nine," Manny said.

"See you in a few minutes then."

The dinner looked dried out—it was left over from two days before. Donald scanned the refrigerator for something to make it more appetizing.

He spread some mustard on the ham and poured Italian dressing on the spaghetti and mixed it around. Then he put it in the microwave and cut up an orange.

"Good to go," he said to the cat.

He was still eating when Manny arrived.

"Want to watch TV?" Donald asked.

"Nah. I was thinking we should play Monopoly. We haven't done that in at least a year."

So Donald climbed the stairs to his room and got the game. He also unplugged his radio and brought that down.

"What the heck is this?" Manny asked as a gruff, heavy voice on the radio started singing about a ring of fire.

"Sounds like Johnny Cash."

Manny winced. "What are we, sixty years old? Put on a good station."

"This *is* good. I listen to this station every night."

"You got weird tastes, man." Manny rolled the dice and moved his little metal boot to Vermont Avenue. "I'll buy that," he said.

Donald also rolled an eight and sighed. First move of the game and he already owed Manny six dollars. "Great start," he said.

"This might be a rout."

"No way," Donald said. "Monopoly is a marathon, not a sprint."

"What do you know about marathons?"

"I know I wouldn't want to run one."

Donald shoveled the last forkful of spaghetti into his mouth and got up to put the plate in the dishwasher.

"What do we have to drink?" Manny asked.

"Apple juice." Donald opened the refrigerator and looked in. "Chocolate milk."

"Could I have some juice?"

"Sure. Oh, and there's half a pot of cold, stale coffee from this morning if you want that."

"No thanks. You go ahead."

Donald rolled his eyes and shook his head. "My dad will microwave it when he gets home from work. Strong black coffee. He lives on the stuff."

"Doesn't it keep him awake?'"

"Not for a second. We don't have any trouble sleeping in this family. Good sleep genes or something."

"No stress?"

"We don't let it get to us. Not usually. Only if one of us has a bad wrestling match."

Manny laughed. "How'd it go today?"

"I beat Mario and lost to Jesse. We got Palisades tomorrow. You going to be there?"

"Yeah. I can run after. You can join me if you need to run out your frustrations again."

"I'm not counting on any frustrations tomorrow. I think I'm ready to win one." Donald rolled the dice and landed on Indiana, which Manny had just purchased.

"You're not winning this one," Manny said with glee. "That'll be eighteen bucks."

Donald tossed the bills across the board. "Just wait until I buy Boardwalk and Park Place. You'll be sorry."

"I'm scared, buddy." Manny looked over at the radio, which was playing "Mess Around" by Ray Charles. "You gotta be kidding me with this music," he said.

"It grows on you."

Donald rolled a six and moved his metal wheelbarrow forward. "Finally!" he said, landing on Marvin Gardens. "I'll buy that one." He rubbed his palms together. "I'd say I'm back in business."

It was nearly nine thirty when Donald's mom got home from work.

"No sign of Dad yet," Donald said as he hugged her in the hallway.

"He's working until midnight so he can leave early tomorrow to see your wrestling thing."

"Great."

"How was the dinner?"

"Not bad. I souped it up a little. I like to improvise, you know."

"So I've noticed."

"Manny came over."

"That's good."

"I kicked his butt in Monopoly."

Mrs. Jenkins shook her head with a wry smile. "You boys are so competitive."

"I know. We can't help it."

He sat with his mom while she ate her dinner, then he went upstairs to shower and go to bed. Tomorrow was huge, and he wanted to be rested.

But it took him nearly two hours to fall asleep. And even then he kept dreaming that he was in a half nelson, his shoulders being forced toward the mat. The mat was a giant Monopoly board. Everyone in the bleachers was calling him a loser.

He woke up in a sweat and looked out the window.

The match was still fifteen hours away.

12

The Pressure Builds

"You don't have much to say, huh?" Manny asked after they'd walked most of the way to school in silence.

"Too much in my head," Donald replied. "Just thinking about the match."

"I been there," Manny said. "Pre-event jitters."

"This is like pre-event flu or something. Way beyond jitters."

"You'll survive."

They entered the school and went straight for their lockers, where a group of guys always gathered in the minutes before the bell. Calvin and

Anthony and Kendrick were there, laughing about something that had happened in a class the day before.

Donald grabbed his books and walked straight toward his homeroom.

"Where are you going?" Anthony called. "What, do we have bad breath or something?"

Donald turned and smirked at him. "Of course you do. But I have to finish some homework. I'll see you later."

That was a lie. His homework was all done, but he was in no mood for joking around this morning. Tonight. After the match. He'd be feeling better by then.

As long as he won, that is.

Donald carried his lunch bag across the cafeteria and sat near the trash cans with his back to the room. Manny and Calvin and Anthony were at their usual table, but Donald couldn't bring himself to join them. He slowly chewed his peanut-butter sandwich and stared at the wall.

He had no appetite, but he knew he'd have to force this sandwich down. He was already a nervous wreck; he didn't need to be weak and under-fueled, too.

All around him kids were talking and laughing, relieved to have a break from the classroom. A few people said hello, but Donald just grunted or nodded back.

He just might get pinned again this afternoon. Maybe he was kidding himself to think otherwise. He opened his math book and laid it flat, pretending to be studying. But every thought he had was about wrestling.

After a few minutes he glanced around; everybody was emptying their trays and getting ready to go back to class. The clock said 11:55. Four more hours until the match.

Donald hustled into math class seconds before the bell rang. He could feel Mrs. Epstein's eyes on him. He looked up as she made a notation on her attendance sheet.

Kendrick tossed a crumpled piece of paper at Donald, hitting him in the arm. "How come you snubbed us at lunch?" he asked.

Donald shrugged. "Just wanted to be alone."

"Why?"

"You know. The match."

"That's three hours away."

"Think I don't know that? I've been counting the hours since yesterday."

"I try not to think about it."

"I can't do anything but."

Mrs. Epstein cleared her throat. Donald turned to face the front of the classroom. But he spent most of the period staring at his notebook, where he'd written a single word: FINISH!

What a relief it was to get to the locker room. He hadn't paid attention in any of his classes. Now he could fully concentrate on the task at hand.

He put on his uniform and his warm-up suit, then took his headgear from his locker. There was still a good hour before the match would begin, but at least there were no more distractions.

They warmed up as a team, with Tavo and Freddy leading the stretching and limbering. Then Coach gathered them back in the locker room for a pep talk and strategy session.

Donald would be up first again. His match didn't count in the team scoring, but it still meant a huge deal to him. This wasn't practice. The boys in the blue uniforms were invaders in the Hudson City gym.

He waved to his father, who had just entered the gym and was heading toward the bleachers. Dad raised his fist and mouthed, "Good luck."

Donald stretched his arms high overhead, then slowly reached for his toes. He looked across the gym. Warming up behind the Palisades bench was a short wrestler with wide shoulders and an expression that seemed to say *TOUGH* in capital letters. That was the guy he'd be wrestling. It had to be.

Donald swallowed hard. In a couple more minutes he'd be out there.

It was time to find out what he was made of.

13

Music

Donald took a deep breath and shut his eyes. When he opened them, that Palisades wrestler was still staring him down from across the mat as they waited for the referee to call them out.

Coach put a hand on Donald's shoulder. "Ready?" he asked.

"You know it." He bounced up and down a few times, shaking out his wrists and knees.

Donald glanced at the bleachers. There were a lot more spectators than last time; the place was more than half full. Manny and Anthony were seated in the top row. His father was about half-way up.

The referee waved them onto the mat and made them shake hands. The guy's grip was strong and dry, but he only held it for a fraction of a second. He never took his eyes off Donald's.

And though he was short with a stocky wrestler's build, his style did not seem conventional at all. His stance was very low and somewhat off center, as if he was leaning to his left. And his feet kept moving side to side as he circled around Donald. He didn't offer much of a target.

Donald crouched lower, too, but after thirty seconds of moving around like that, his legs felt pretty darn tired. So he stood up straighter and darted to the side. And that's when the guy attacked.

Head down, he wrapped his arms around Donald's legs and tried to lift them both. Donald reached down to grab his shoulders and twisted his own body, but the guy had a very strong grip. There was no place to go but down. Donald was behind, 2–0.

No panic, Donald thought. *You'll figure this guy out.*

He got to his knees, but the guy had one arm around his waist and the other had a tight grip on his shoulder. It took him nearly a minute to wiggle out of the hold, getting to his feet and jumping free.

The period was winding down, but Donald was not about to stand around and wait. The Palisades wrestler was finally standing straight, so Donald made the big penetrating step and shot in low, wrapping both hands around his opponent's knee. He lifted and turned, bringing the guy down flat on the mat and coming up behind him.

Instinctively Donald hooked his left arm under his opponent's arm and reached up behind his head. He drove hard with his legs to turn the guy toward his back.

"Half nelson!" shouted Tavo. "You got him."

Donald could tell that he had him now. He'd been on the wrong side of this move enough times to recognize when the outcome was certain. The

Palisades wrestler was straining, pushing with everything he had, but Donald had a lock-tight grip and all of the momentum. He was slowly forcing the guy's shoulders toward the mat.

And within seconds Donald felt the momentum stop, felt the hard resistance of the mat pressing up against those shoulders. This guy was pinned.

The referee slapped the mat.

It was the best sound Donald had ever heard.

He leaped to his feet and pumped his fist. He shook hands with the Palisades wrestler. The referee raised Donald's arm as the victor.

Coach got him in a quick headlock and said, "Beautiful job. You're on your way, kid."

Tavo smacked his arm, and Freddy met Donald's fist with his own. Donald pulled off his headgear and looked around the gym.

Here came his dad, stepping down from the bleachers. He reached over and shook Donald's hand. "Way to go, Darnald. That was fun."

"Sure was," Donald said. "It's great that you got here."

"It was worth the hassle." Dad looked at his watch. "Wish I could stay for the rest, but I'm due back at work for a couple more hours."

"I know. I'll see you tonight."

Donald walked to the locker room, way too excited to take a seat with the others yet. Incredibly, he had even more energy now than he'd had before the match.

He bounced up and down in front of his locker, throwing out his fists like a boxer. What a difference a win made. He felt like he could wrestle five more matches and still have energy to burn.

Kendrick and Mario also won their prelims, and Hudson City dominated the varsity match. So there were a lot of happy, rowdy wrestlers in the locker room afterward.

"Pizza," Kendrick said with a big smile. "We earned it."

"Villa Roma," Donald replied. "I told Manny we'd meet him at seven."

"Good deal. I gotta run home and get some money."

Donald looked around at the other wrestlers. This felt more like a team now, more than just eighth-graders ruling over seventh-graders. They'd come a long way in less than a month. He was glad to be a part of it.

Wrestling was hard, but it was worth it. He had no doubts about that now.

Donald stepped out of the gym with his head held high, walking across the dark pavement. Since he'd started wrestling he hadn't seen much daylight except on the weekends. School until three, then practice or matches until well after dark. It was six o'clock already.

He was hungry, but he had at least an hour to kill before Manny or Kendrick or anyone else would show up at Villa Roma. So he headed toward the Boulevard and turned right. There was a store down there that he wanted to check out: *Lindo Música Internacional.*

He'd been in here a few times, so he knew they

had what he wanted. He nodded to the man behind the counter and walked past racks of CDs toward the back, where a few guitars hung from the wall.

"Help you?" asked the salesman, who had followed him down the aisle. The man was thin with a neatly trimmed dark mustache.

"Maybe." Donald pointed toward the ceiling, though he wasn't sure where the music was coming from. "What's this playing?" The song was fast and guitar heavy, and the singing was in Spanish.

"El Torito. They're Dominican."

"Cool. I wanted to look at the guitars."

"Do you play?"

"Not yet."

The man took an acoustic guitar from the wall and handed it to Donald, who plucked one of the strings and listened to it resonate. "Could a person teach himself how to play?" he asked.

The man smiled. "You could. But you'd save a lot of time by taking lessons. There are several people around the neighborhood who give them."

He pointed to a bulletin board on the wall that had small posters announcing where local bands would be performing, a few business cards for DJ services for weddings and parties, and announcements of bands looking for musicians or singers. The word LESSONS caught Donald's eye. He counted four cards with phone numbers of guitar teachers.

Donald carefully handed the guitar back to the salesman, admiring the smooth grain of the wood and the tautness of the strings. "Christmas is a couple of weeks away. I'll send my dad in."

He'd noticed the price tag on the guitar, though. It was steep. "Do you ever sell used guitars?" he asked.

"Sure. Sometimes." The man put the instrument back in its place. "We have songbooks and picks and anything else you'd need, too."

Donald guessed that even a used guitar of that quality would be expensive. Maybe he could go with a lesser model for now. They probably had some at Kmart. His mother got an employee discount.

"Thanks," Donald said. "I'll definitely be back."

"Anytime," said the man. "We're open late."

The Boulevard was all lit up—Christmas lights overhead and trees and decorations in most of the store windows. People were walking quickly, carrying packages and shopping bags and take-out food from the Mexican and Asian restaurants.

He still had a lot of time. His mouth watered when he walked past La Isla Café and smelled the food. Villa Roma's pizza would be a very welcome gift to his stomach.

Donald felt warm in his hooded sweatshirt and windbreaker, relaxed and happy from the visit to the music store, and confident and excited about his success on the wrestling mat. Things were looking good. And he knew they'd continue to get better.

He walked past the Y and turned up Ninth Street past St. Joseph's Church toward the high-school athletic fields, then back along Central Avenue, just wandering.

He had time to kill. He was in no hurry, just

enjoying some freedom and his own company. There'd be plenty of noise and joking around at the pizza place. This quiet walk was another time to savor, like lying in bed at night with the radio.

For the next little while, Donald had no particular destination. But one thing he knew for certain: He was headed in the right direction.

★ ★ ★

Read an excerpt from
CURVEBALL
Winning Season #9

Eddie Ventura scanned the infield, then dug his toe into the dirt near first base. His right hand was sweating inside his glove despite the cool afternoon breeze.

Everyone in the dugout and the bleachers was standing, waiting for Ramiro Velez to deliver the crucial pitch.

Eddie took a deep breath and went into a crouch, ready to dart toward any ball that was hit or thrown his way. The Hudson City Hornets had to get this next hitter out.

"Let's go, Ramiro!" Eddie called. "No batter!"

Ramiro turned his head slightly toward Eddie, and a faint smile crossed his lips. Eddie hardly ever said anything.

Hoboken had runners at second and third with two outs in the top of the final inning. Hudson City would get one more at-bat, but the Hornets were already two runs behind.

Ramiro leaned back, kicked up his leg, and hurled the ball toward the plate. The batter swung hard, but the ball smacked into catcher Jared Owen's mitt for strike three.

Ramiro shook his fist.

"Yes!" said Eddie as they raced off the field.

"Big rally now," Spencer Lewis said to Eddie as they grabbed their bats from the rack. "We need some base runners."

Spencer was the team's best hitter and biggest talker, but the Hornets needed to get at least two men on base or Spencer wouldn't even bat.

And things didn't look good as Willie Shaw popped the first pitch lazily toward second base. Eddie groaned with the rest of the Hornets as the fielder easily caught the ball.

Lamont Wilkins struck out, and just like that the Hornets were down to their last out.

Jared stepped up to the plate. Eddie shut his eyes quickly, then moved to the on-deck circle.

Relax, Eddie told himself. *Time to do something big here.*

Eddie was a fair hitter—a lefty—but no way was he one of the stars. He'd had three singles in the first six games and had drawn a couple of walks. But he'd never been one to really come through in the clutch the way Spencer or Jared always seemed to.

The Hornets had lost their first four games this season, but they were presently riding a modest two-game winning streak. A third straight victory today would be an enormous boost, but a loss would put them back in a deep hole.

Eddie's tall, thin build didn't provide much power, except in his imagination. *On deck for the Hudson City Hornets—EDDIEEE Ven-TUR-a,* he thought, sounding to himself like one of the broadcasters for the New York Yankees. *If Jared can get on base here, the hard-hitting Ventura will surely make something happen.*

A burst of cheers broke Eddie from his thoughts,

and he looked up to see Jared sprinting toward first base. Eddie gripped the bat tighter.

Jared rounded first and kept on going, sliding safely into second with a double.

Spencer stepped out of the dugout and gave Eddie a firm punch on the shoulder. "Grind time, Mr. Ventura," Spencer said. "It's up to you now, boss."

Eddie swallowed hard. He walked to the plate and took a practice swing. He heard that imaginary radio voice again: *Ventura could homer and tie this game with one swing of the bat.* But then again, he'd never hit a home run in his life.

The pitcher took the throw from the second baseman and turned to face Eddie. He squinted and glared. Eddie glared back, trying to look tougher than he felt.

This guy had struck Eddie out twice today. He had a wicked fastball and a decent curve. But he had to be tiring by now.

Jared took a short lead off second base. Eddie drew back his bat and waited. The first pitch was low and outside. Ball one.

"Good eye, Eddie!" came a cry.

The second pitch was high and outside. Eddie stepped out of the batter's box and glanced toward the Hornets' dugout.

"A walk's as good as a hit," Coach Wimmer called.

Eddie let out his breath. It was true. He didn't need a home run. He didn't even need a single. All he had to do was get on base and keep this inning alive.

Eddie crouched a little lower and inched closer to the plate, trying to shrink his strike zone. The third pitch looked good, maybe a little low, but right down the center of the plate.

Eddie didn't flinch. The umpire called, "Ball three!" and the pitcher shook his head in frustration.

The Hoboken catcher turned to the umpire.

"It was low," the umpire said.

The catcher called time and jogged to the mound to talk to the pitcher. Eddie's teammates were rattling the fence in front of their dugout. Spencer was grinning confidently at Eddie from the on-deck circle. "Gut check!" Spencer said. "Be the man."

Eddie wiped his sweaty palms on his uniform pants. A hundred things crossed his mind at once. Nobody swung on a 3–0 count, so the pitcher would be playing it safe. He'd groove one right down the middle. Eddie could bunt it, then run like mad toward first base.

Or, he thought, *This kid Ventura has the ability to hit away, driving the ball deep into the outfield and bringing Jared home.*

Or he could play it safe, too, like he knew he was supposed to. Take the pitch even if it was a strike.

And here it came, waist-high but inside. Eddie leaned back as the ball whizzed by.

"Ball four," called the umpire. "Take your base."

Eddie couldn't help but smile as he jogged toward first. The dugout fence was shaking and rattling again; Miguel and Lamont and the others were yelling his name.

The Hoboken coach walked to the mound and chatted with the pitcher, but he left him in the game.

Eddie stepped off first base, tensed and ready

to sprint all the way home if he needed to.

Here came the pitch, here came the *smack* as Spencer connected, the *Oooh* from the spectators, and the roar from the Hudson City dugout as the ball shot deep into right field. Eddie ran hard, but he turned slightly to watch as the ball sailed over the fence and into the parking lot.

That's gone! said the announcer in his mind.

Eddie threw his arms straight over his head and laughed as he stepped on second base. He watched Jared leap onto home plate, then rounded third and raced home to do the same. And with all of his teammates, he waited for Spencer and his enormous, triumphant grin.

They mobbed him. Three straight wins. The Hornets were definitely back in business.

RICH WALLACE

was a high school and college athlete and then a sportswriter before he began writing novels. He is the author of many critically acclaimed sports-themed novels, including *Wrestling Sturbridge*, *Shots on Goal*, and *Restless: A Ghost's Story*. Wallace lives with his family in Honesdale, Pennsylvania.